LORENZO

Written and Illustrated by

David McPhail

Doubleday & Company, Inc.
Garden City, New York

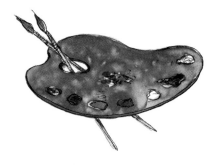

Library of Congress Cataloging in Publication Data

McPhail, David M.   Lorenzo.

Summary: Lorenzo, a traveling artist, moves into a deserted home in a hollow
tree and makes friends with his neighbors, the forest animals.
[1. Artists—Fiction.   2. Animals—Friction.   3. Dwellings—Fiction]   I. Title.
PZ7.M2427Lo   [E]   AACR2

ISBN: 0-385-15590-5 Trade
ISBN: 0-385-15591-3 Prebound
Library of Congress Catalog Card Number 79-7871

Lorenzo

Lorenzo was an artist.
He went
from place to place,
painting pictures
and selling them.

On his back
Lorenzo carried a pack.
In the pack were Lorenzo's
paints and brushes.

Lorenzo liked being outdoors.
He liked to paint
pictures of trees and birds
and other things
that he saw
as he went along.

At night Lorenzo
slept in a pile of leaves
on the ground.
That was fun
when he was young.
But he was not young anymore.

He wished he had a house
with a real bed in it.
If he had a house,
he could hang up
some of his pictures, too.
So Lorenzo decided to
save his money
and buy a house.

One day a man
asked Lorenzo
to paint a picture
of his children.

The man liked the picture.
He gave Lorenzo
some money for it.

A farmer asked him
to paint a picture of his cow.

The farmer liked the picture, but
he did not have any money.
He gave Lorenzo some milk instead.
Lorenzo was thirsty.
He drank all the milk.

Lorenzo was hungry, too.
He gave his money to the baker.
The baker gave Lorenzo a
loaf of bread.
Lorenzo ate all of the bread.

Now the milk was all gone,
and the bread was all gone,
and his money was all gone.
Lorenzo was sad.
How could he buy a house
if he had no money?

It was getting late.
Lorenzo was very tired.
He walked into the forest
to find a place to sleep.

He found a big tree.
Lorenzo leaned against it
and fell asleep.
In the morning, when
Lorenzo woke up,
he noticed something very strange.

There was a little window
in the side of the tree.

Lorenzo looked in the window.
There was a little room
with a bed in it.

Lorenzo went around
to the other side
of the tree.
He found a little door.
He knocked on the door.
There was no answer.
He knocked again.

"There is no one home,"
someone said.
"No one lives there anymore."
Lorenzo looked around.
He could not see anyone.

"Down here," said the voice.
Lorenzo looked down.
A mole was standing there.

"I'm Mole," said the mole.
"And I'm Lorenzo," said Lorenzo.
"Glad to meet you."

"Clifton Badger
used to live here,"
Mole told Lorenzo.
"But he went away.
I don't think
he will ever
be back."

Mole pushed open the door
and went in.
"Follow me," he said.

It was very low inside.
Lorenzo almost bumped his head.

There was a kitchen
and a bedroom
and a living room.

Lorenzo saw many places
to hang his paintings.

"Would you like to
live here?" Mole asked Lorenzo.
"Yes," said Lorenzo.
"But I can't buy a house.
I don't have any money."

"You don't need
money," Mole said.
"No one in the forest
needs money."

Lorenzo was happy.
He took some paintings
out of his pack and hung them
on the walls.

Then he sat down
in a soft chair.
"Lorenzo, the Artist, finally
has a home," he said to Mole.

Lorenzo at Home

Lorenzo liked
his new home.

In the morning
he ate his breakfast
in the kitchen.

And everyday he went for a walk.
He said "Hello"
to everyone he met.

When he got back
from his walk,
Lorenzo painted
some pictures.

After supper
Lorenzo read a book
until bedtime.
"This is so fine,"
he would say
as he fell asleep.

The Garden

Lorenzo wanted to plant
a garden, but he didn't
know what to do first.

Lorenzo's friend, Mole,
came to help.

"First you dig up
the ground," said Mole.
Mole and Lorenzo
dug the garden
together.

When they were done,
they planted
some seeds.

"I will get some water,"
said Lorenzo
when the garden
was all planted.
He took his water can
and walked to a nearby well.

Lorenzo was gone a long time.
"I wonder where Lorenzo is,"
said Mole.
Mole went to look
for Lorenzo.

He walked to the well.
He found Lorenzo's
water can, but he did not
find Lorenzo.
"Lorenzo!" called Mole.
But there was no answer.
"Lorenzo!" Mole
called again, louder.

This time
Lorenzo answered.
But he sounded
very far away.
Mole looked
all around.
Then he looked
down the well.

There was Lorenzo
at the bottom
of the well.

"What are you
doing down there?"
asked Mole.

"I fell in!"
said Lorenzo.
"Please get me out!"
"I will try," said Mole,
but he could not reach
the handle.
"I will untie
the rope and
pull you out," said Mole.

"Don't untie the rope,
Mole," shouted Lorenzo.
"If you do, I will fall
back in the . . ."

SPLASH!
Too late.
"Is the water deep?"
Mole asked.
"No," said Lorenzo,
"but it is cold!"

"Hold on!"
said Mole,
as he pulled
on the rope.

But Lorenzo was
too heavy.
"I will get help,"
said Mole.
Mole found two
rabbits to help.

Mole and the two rabbits
pulled on the rope.
They pulled and
they pulled, but
they could not
pull Lorenzo out
of the well.

A little mouse
picked up the rope
and pulled.
The rabbits laughed
at the mouse,
but Mole saw the rope move.

"The mouse is pulling
Lorenzo out of the
well!" said Mole.
"Let's help!"
Mole and the two rabbits
helped the little mouse
pull Lorenzo out of the well.

"Thank you so much,"
said Lorenzo.

Then he went into his
house to change his clothes.

When Lorenzo got back
to the garden,
Mole was still there.
"Now I will get
some water
for the garden,"
said Lorenzo.

"Be careful, Lorenzo,"
said Mole.
"I will be careful, Mole,"
said Lorenzo.

Lorenzo was gone
a long time.
"I wonder what happened
to Lorenzo?" said Mole.

The Visitor

One day there was
a loud knock at the door.
Lorenzo went to the door
and opened it.
Standing there was Mole.
"Clifton Badger is
coming!" Mole puffed.
"I just saw him
walking along the path!"
"I hope that he
will visit," said Lorenzo.

"Visit!" cried Mole.
"He might do more
than visit! He might
want his house back!"

"Now, Mole," said Lorenzo.
"Calm down."
But Mole was too excited
to calm down.

"This is *your* house
now, Lorenzo," said Mole.
"And I'm going to tell
him so!"

"No," said Lorenzo.
"You run along home
and calm yourself down."
Lorenzo gently pushed
Mole out the door
and closed it.

A moment later
there was another knock
at the door.
"Now, Mole," said Lorenzo
as he opened the door.
"I told you—"
And he stopped.
For it wasn't a mole
standing there
at all . . .
It was a badger!

"You must be Clifton Badger,"
said Lorenzo.
"That's right," said the badger.
"And who are you?"
"My name is Lorenzo," said Lorenzo.
"Please come in."

Clifton followed Lorenzo
into the kitchen,
where Lorenzo made some tea
and warmed some biscuits.

"I was just going by,"
said Clifton, "and I wanted
to see my old house."
"It's the first
house I ever lived in,"
said Lorenzo.
"I love to travel," said Clifton,
"after so many years
in this house."
"And I love being in
this house," said Lorenzo,
"after so many years of
traveling."

"I wish I could stay
longer," Clifton
said to Lorenzo
when the biscuits
were all gone.
"But I must be on my way."
Lorenzo took a small
painting down from the
wall and handed it to
Clifton.

"It's a picture of *our* house,"
said Lorenzo.
"I want you to have it."
"Thank you," said Clifton.
"It's a very nice picture."

When Clifton Badger left,
Mole returned.
"Does Clifton want his
house back?" asked Mole.
"No," said Lorenzo.
"He is happy traveling."
"Then you don't have to move!"
shouted Mole.
"That's right," said Lorenzo,
and he smiled.

A long silent moment
passed. Then Mole spoke.
"Well, if you *did* have to move,"
he told Lorenzo, "you could have
moved in with me."

"Thank you, Mole,"
said Lorenzo. And he
thought of Mole's
very tiny house.
"It's good to have
a friend like you."

THE END